Craven House
Horrors

PLOT YOUR OWN
HORROR STORIES™ #1

Craven House Horrors

By HILARY MILTON

WANDERER BOOKS
Published by Simon & Schuster, New York

Copyright © 1982 by Hilary Milton
All rights reserved
including the right of reproduction
in whole or in part in any form
Published by WANDERER BOOKS
A Simon & Schuster Division of
Gulf & Western Corporation
Simon & Schuster Building
1230 Avenue of the Americas
New York, New York 10020

Designed by Stanley S. Drate

Manufactured in the United States of America

10 9 8 7 6 5 4 3 2 1

WANDERER and colophon are trademarks
of Simon & Schuster
Library of Congress Cataloging in Publication Data

Milton, Hilary H.
  Craven House horrors.

  (Plot your own horror stories; 1)
  Summary: Trapped by a storm in a mysterious and
frightening house, the reader is given several
alternative choices to manipulate the plot and plan
an escape.
  [1. Horror—Fiction. 2. Literary recreations]
I. Title. II. Series.
PZ7.M6447Cr 1981   [Fic]   82-7020
ISBN 0-671-45631-8   AACR2

BEWARE!

Craven House is filled with unnatural horror. You'll struggle desperately to survive your stay there. Don't read straight through, however, as every time you think you're safe, a new and frightening choice will have to be made.

Should you follow the jeering black bird?
Is the young girl an innocent victim . . or a calculating witch?
Will you be able to outsmart the evil creature that is stalking you?

Remember, your fate is in your own hands. Only you can decide whether or not you'll make it through the many tales of terror in *Craven House Horrors!*

It is late afternoon on a Saturday in March. You have spent the day with your cousins Jane and Eric. The three of you have stayed almost the entire day in the paddock behind the barn, riding Eric's new pony. You are standing off to one side while Eric holds the lead rope when Aunt Marsha comes to the back door and calls you. "Your mother just phoned," she says. "She wants you to come home immediately—there's a terrible storm brewing."

You say good-bye to your cousins, slip on your jacket, and climb onto your bicycle. Home is four miles away and you surely don't want to get caught in the storm.

It wouldn't be four miles, you think, if you could use Willow Lane. That route would cut the distance to less than three miles. But you aren't supposed to use Willow Lane. Nobody is supposed to use Willow Lane. Barricades block it at both ends because the owner of the ancient Craven House says the road belongs to him—that's what the story is in North Charleston, at any rate.

2

Anyway, barricades or not, nobody wants to take Willow Lane because it goes past the huge, spooky-looking Craven House.

As you pedal rapidly along the gravel road, you think of all the stories you've heard about the run-down plantation house. It was built more than a hundred years ago, long before the War Between the States. The Craven family was very rich. But with the war, things changed for them. One of the stories is that the younger son went off to fight, was wounded, and returned home to recover. He'd been shot in the head, though, and went crazy—killed his mother and father and ran his older brother and two sisters off the family property.

Another story is that this same son went off to war, got shot, and came home just before Union soldiers invaded the area. He hid in the garret, but his family was forced to move out when the Union general made the house his headquarters. The poor soldier died in the tiny room at the top without anybody knowing he was there.

There's another story, but you don't think much of it. According to this one, the great-grandson of the original owners returned to the house six years ago and now lives in it like a hermit. Some say he's crazy. Some say he's a mad genius. Others say he's an engineer and there are a few who call him a mad doctor. Whatever he might be, however, nobody goes near the house—not even the postman.

You and your cousins really think Willow Lane is blocked off to protect people from the old man.

You don't know whether the stories are true, but right now you wish you didn't have to ride so far with the wind blowing so hard.

When you approach the barricades and are about to ride past, a violent gust of wind blows down a tree, blocking your path. You brake hard to keep from being hit and realize you'll have to take Willow Lane anyway—you can't proceed along Parker Road.

You push your bike around the barricades and start riding as fast as you can. You're not really afraid of the old man in the Craven House but you want to get home before the storm strikes. Trouble is, the lane hasn't been used much and there are potholes and loose gravel trenches—you have to zigzag to dodge them.

You're no more than twenty feet from the path leading to the Craven House, but as you approach it, another violent gust of wind blows across, knocking you and the bicycle over. You fall into a deep ditch beside the lane, and when you climb out you discover that your front wheel is badly bent. You cannot ride at all.

While you're trying to straighten the wheel, the

winds become even stronger, and limbs fall from trees all around you. The rain begins falling, then sweeps across in blinding sheets. Lightning cuts through the dark clouds, and you know you cannot stay where you are. You have to seek shelter.

Mustering your courage, you push the bicycle toward the Craven House porch—you don't plan to go inside but you think you can stay on the porch for a while, maybe until the storm blows over.

The porch floor creaks when you step up onto it, and you know rotten boards are everywhere. Near the front door, however, the floor seems to be stronger so you move toward it.

As you step onto a particularly wide board, the front door swings open.

You really don't mean to do so, but you feel drawn toward the dry room inside, so you step through the opening—just to get out of the storm.

You take three steps, stop, and stare about you, eyes wide with wonder. Heavy, dark chairs and tables are arranged much as you suspect they could have been when the Craven family died—or was forced to leave. Beneath a wide marble mantel, the blackened fireplace hints of fires long ago—except you think you see ashes that couldn't have been left for over a hundred years. Somewhere in another part of the

5

6

house, a machine seems to be running—its deep whir echoes through the room.

And while you're standing there, you hear a soft whisperlike brush. You whirl about—in time to see the door close and latch itself.

Shaking all over, you can't decide what to do— leave, stay right where you are, or seek the source of that noise.

If you choose to leave, turn to page 30.
If you decide to stay right where you are until the storm subsides, turn to page 22.
If you decide to look for the noise's source, turn to page 48.

Terrified by the sound as well as by the threat, you retreat, keeping an eye on the bird and feeling behind you for a chair, a sofa, a table—anything you can hide behind. You've heard how some birds can fly at you, dart down and peck out your eyes.

You find only a small footstool, and you trip over that. You sprawl across the floor, knocking over the footstool and banging into a large floor lamp.

"Flee to be! Flee to be!" the bird chatters.

You duck low. Then you hear the rapid flutter of wings once more.

7

Turn to page 116.

8

You swallow hard and try to step back, knowing you have chosen the wrong door. However, the curtain is no longer soft like cloth but has somehow become heavy and stiff. You cannot part it.

The man slowly turns his massive head and shifts his gaze until the eyes are fixed on you. You cannot tell which part of you he is looking at, though, because you see only yourself mirrored within. But you cannot look long because the strange eyes are like fierce, tiny spotlights. Wordlessly, the man reaches forward and presses a blue button.

Turn to page 21.

9

"Flee! Be free!"

You don't like the sound of the bird's croaking voice and without waiting longer, you turn from the door and scurry to the room's far end. Heavy drapes suggest another opening and you brush the thick cloth out of the way. You find a wide, open stairway leading to a narrow balcony that appears to extend through the wall. You scramble up the steps, turn, and dart across the narrow way. As you duck through a low passageway, you suddenly find yourself in a massive, very dusty bedroom. The tall four-poster bed is covered with a scarlet blanket, and the drooping canopy seems to be sagging with accumulated dust. As you sweep toward the window at the far side, you stir clouds of choking dust. And suddenly your attention is drawn to a lump in the middle of the bed.

You stare—and tremble all over. For there, its shaggy gray hair spread over the dust-laden pillow, is the figure of an old man.

If you choose to leave the room, turn to page 17.
If you stop to check the man's condition, turn to page 79.

10

After several minutes of fruitless searching, you turn to the nearest window. You rub your hand over its surface, wondering if it would be a bad idea to break through. But you discover it is not made of glass. Instead, you find that it is a kind of plexiglass, like the material used in airplane windows. You cannot break it without a hammer.

You stand there for a moment, then decide that since nobody has appeared, there must not be anyone at home. You feel relieved and decide you might as well find a chair and rest until the storm ends.

The heavy furniture is covered with sheets so you walk over to the fireplace and look at the low metal-framed chair at its side. It may not be the most comfortable, but sitting in it will beat standing— you're tired from playing all day and then riding here.

You ease yourself into the chair, discover it has a springy bottom, and stretch out. You place your hands on the arms and lean your head back. You close your eyes—

Turn to page 105.

Swiftly he places a viselike mechanical arm on the front wheel, holds the rest of the bicycle over the desk, and lets it come to rest on the surface. From a small box he brings out two very strange-looking tools—unlike any you've ever seen before—and in the twinkling of an eye he has made the repair. Without a word he places the bicycle on the floor and motions for you to climb onto it.

11

You thank him and do as he says. You test the wheel, the handlebar, the brakes, and the pedals. It makes you feel happy, knowing it is repaired.

The man does not speak. Instead, he turns and points toward a wide curtain. You understand and are glad to be on your way home. Even though you know it isn't proper to ride a bicycle in a house, you think he means for you to ride off.

Turn to page 114.

12

You stop abruptly and glance back at the robot. It hasn't moved from the stove. You look toward the refrigerator door and the soft sound comes again—from inside the huge appliance.

Cautiously you cross to it and grab the great handle. It is hard to open but when you tug firmly it yields. Inside, you see rows of boxes—long boxes that must hold frozen food. There is barely enough light to see, but as you peer inside, you catch a glimpse of a small girl! She is sitting on the floor, all hunched over, her chin resting on her drawn-up knees, her hair falling about her face. Tears streak her cheeks—they look like small icicles.

When she hears the door open, she looks up dumbly. Her eyes are red and you know she has been crying a long time. But she is nearly frozen.

Without thinking, you rush inside and bend over. She tries to reach for your hand but can barely move. You clutch her wrist, pull her up, and drag her out of the refrigerator. As you are about to close the door, she says, "Please," and points at one of her shoes, left where she'd been huddled.

You release her wrist, turn, and start back for the shoe. But as you step within the refrigerator you have a second thought: a trap.

Turn to page 111.

She screams a sound that freezes you in your tracks. You look back—and wish you had not.

She stares straight into your face. Her eyes fix on yours, and those dreaded beams of light blink and blink at your pupils. You very slowly shift until you face her directly. You are being hypnotized. You know it, but you cannot do anything to stop it.

When you are totally still, when you cannot move a muscle, she screams that blood-chilling scream once more. Extending the arm with the snake coiled about it, she commences to hum doleful music.

Bit by bit, the snake's head stretches. Its body slides through her fingers. And for a reason you cannot guess, it becomes stiff as an arrow.

13

Turn to page 15.

The girl lets the snake continue to stretch forward. And when the head is within inches of your bare arm, she thrusts it forward. The mouth springs open, then closes instantly—with the fangs clamped in your flesh.

15

You sting all over, tingling with the pain. But you cannot turn away, cannot run, cannot take a single step.

Slowly you feel yourself slumping to the floor.

THE END

16

The stew has a very strange smell and you really do not want to eat it. But you don't want to anger your host.

You dip your spoon into the bowl, stare at the contents a moment, then put the spoon into your mouth.

Instantly your tongue burns, your eyes water, and your throat feels as if it has been painted with vile acid.

The pain is so great you cannot move.

The little girl gets up, takes the spoon from your paralyzed hand, and dips it into your bowl. Smiling, she places the spoon once again in your mouth.

"It's good for you," she says softly.

THE END

Whirling around, you spy a double door on the opposite side of the room. You dash toward it, bang it open, and dart through—and onto the landing of yet another set of stairs.

Taking the steps two at a time, you plunge back to the main floor of the house. You cross another landing, this one wider than the one on the upper floor, and enter a room bare of furniture. It contains only four gray statues. Two are of men, one is of a woman, and the last is of a child.

The old man who owns Craven House is not only an electronic genius (if the rumor is true). For if these are his works, he is also a master sculptor. You move closer to the first statue. It is a man wearing some kind of uniform, that of a policeman, you think. But the figure is so lifelike you cannot be sure that it is *only* a statue.

You extend a trembling hand to touch the surface. It is smooth, much too smooth to be stone. You bend close to study the material and discover it's some kind of clay.

You touch the outstretched fingers. They are warm!

Turn to page 18.

18

They cannot be warm. But they are.

You squeeze one finger. The clay flecks in your grasp. And before you know it, all the clay falls from the hand. And it *is* a hand—the hand of a policeman. You can see the ring he's wearing!

If you choose to chip away more clay, turn to page 110.
If you think it wiser to run, turn to page 86.

19

Without hesitating, you turn toward the one to the left and step through it. The narrow door slams shut behind you and you find yourself in a space no larger than a telephone booth. The minute you're inside, it begins to move. It goes up, like a tiny elevator. It rises and rises, then suddenly stops. The moment it's still, you scramble out.

You can't be sure, but you think you're in a dimly lit storage attic.

You squint your eyes and stare around—and suddenly discover that you're surrounded by weird, headless stuffed animals. Before you can take another step you hear a sound coming from one of the creatures. You turn quickly. Slowly ambling toward you, as if it could see, as if it could attack, is the huge, muscular body of a lion. You holler and try to back away.

Turn to page 63.

20

You try to scream but your throat is too tight.

And while you can do nothing more than stand there, frozen in place, the thing's grotesque arms slowly reach for you. They press against your sides and the barbs gouge through your shirt, into your skin. Like huge needles, they prick you in a hundred places. And the tingling becomes so violent that your body shakes all over.

"Flesh for the stingers."

You don't know where the voice came from, but it doesn't matter. You are lifted off the surface and turned as the thing turns. It holds you dangling and kicking and slowly proceeds to carry you toward an unimaginable end.

Within less than a minute it stops and pivots to the left. Shaking all over, you glance down.

You're suspended over a huge pit. At the bottom are swarms of giant ants, each one bigger than a rat.

And the thing slowly releases its grip.

THE END

Instantly small glowing lights illuminate two walls. You stare at them. Both are lined with wide shelves. Along one, you spot small toylike vehicles—automobiles, pickup trucks, motorcycles, bikes, and even boats. As your glance shifts from one to the next, you realize there's something peculiar about them.

21

Turn to page 40.

22

You stand motionless for a moment, listening for any sounds that may help you make up your mind. But you hear nothing more and decide that the gusting winds caused the door to close.

You stare about the dim room and hope that all the stories you've heard are just that—stories and nothing more. The storm is blowing harder, the wind is causing tree limbs to brush harshly against the side of the house, and the pounding rain sounds like loose pebbles clacking against the windows.

Suddenly, a tiny light startles you and you quickly glance up at the mantel. A low blue flame has appeared on one of the tall candles. Within seconds another, then another, then more than you can count come to life. The room is at once illuminated by the small, flickering glows.

Continue.

Before you have time to react, you hear a sudden flapping noise. You spin about in time to see the largest black bird you've ever seen fly through the doorway from the next room. It glides past you and alights at the top of a tall coatrack near the door. It settles on one foot, turns about, and cocks its head in your direction. Will it attack you? Or merely sit there and stare?

23

If you think the bird will attack, turn to page 36.
If you believe it will simply sit, turn to page 42.

24

The egg cracks for a fourth time, and all at once the fragments fall away. Something begins to emerge.

It looks something like a lizard or a horned frog. Or maybe one of those things called a Gila monster, those poisonous creatures that live out West.

It begins to crawl toward you, growing larger as it moves. Its long, flicking tongue darts in and out of a small mouthlike opening.

All you want to do is slip through a gap in the bars and escape. Except the bars are too close together; the spaces are too narrow.

Turn to page 26.

26

There's nothing at hand to fight the creature off with, and you know that if it bites you, it will kill you. You sniff hard and yell at the thing. But the tongue keeps flicking in and out; the head bobs from side to side.

You think hard, remembering all the pictures of prehistoric lizards you've seen in the encyclopedia. And you recall one special feature—all of them had fat, soft-looking bellies.

Turn to page 84.

The girl seems to be as surprised to see you as you are to see her. She sits upright, her green eyes fixed on you, and eases to the edge of the chair. "Who—who are you?" Her voice is deeper than you expect.

"I—I want to get away from here," you say.

Her little feet reach down until her toes are touching the floor. Her body stiffens, as if she doubts what you say. Then, with an abrupt turn, she flings herself off the chair and runs screaming down the hallway.

"I won't hurt you!" you yell.

She goes to the far end of the hallway and darts around a corner. Without thinking, you trot after her. But just as you reach the corner and turn, you stop suddenly. She is standing beside a low counter, holding in her hand a writhing snake. There is no longer a smile on her face. Her eyes are squinting and from them come green, darting rays of light. Her lips

27

Turn to page 28.

28 are drawn back to reveal even teeth on the bottom and sides—and two fangs that extend to her lower lip. The smooth face is now wrinkled, and her golden curls have become tangled silver-gray webs.

The snake coils itself about her arm, its head caught between her thumb and forefinger, its stem-like tongue darting in and out.

If you believe she'll thrust the snake toward you, turn to page 13.
If you think she'll do something else, turn to page 45.

The big black bird!

"Intruder! Intruder! Flee for your life! You'll die! You'll die! You'll die!"

You don't know whether to fight off the bird or continue your climb.

You hesitate only a split second, then continue up the stairs with the bird still perched on your head.

Turn to page 46.

30

You hear the noise getting louder and decide it must be the man who owns the house. If you go looking for him and he doesn't like it, he might call the police—if he has a telephone. Or he might hold you prisoner until someone comes looking for you.

The porch is getting wet, you know, but there's a wide overhang and if you stay close to the main wall, you'll avoid the worst of the storm. You're not so sure about the old man—those weird stories and all.

You turn and tiptoe to the front door. Glancing around to make sure nobody has heard you, you fumble for the door handle. You can't find it and turn to look. There isn't one; there is no inside handle at all!

You bend over to study the crack between the door and the frame and discover a dead-bolt lock that seems not to have a key. You fumble in your jeans pocket, hoping you have a piece of wire or a strong toothpick. No such luck. You study the door again, looking for a secret button that will push the bolt back. You can't find anything.

Is there an open or unlocked window? Turn to page 10.
Do you look for something in the room to use in forcing the bolt? Turn to page 41.

But you don't care. You're away from the gruesome skeleton, out of the narrow stairway. You glance up as the bird glides off, then swings about and returns. It hovers above your head. "Flee! Be free!"

"Which way?" you ask, realizing you're talking to the creature but hoping it can understand.

It does not answer. Instead, it flies off toward the distant end of the hallway. You trot after it. You come to a sudden left turn—and the glimmers of light from the candle suddenly vanish. It is as if they've all been blown out.

"Flee! Be free!"

The bird is somewhere ahead but in the darkness you cannot see it. You pause long enough to get your bearings. And as you stare forward, you see two tiny spots of light, very close together. The bird's eyes!

But even while you stare they grow and grow. They look like two green Christmas tree lights, then like the beams of two strange flashlights, then like automobile headlights, getting larger and farther apart.

They seem to be coming toward you. And the sound you hear is not at all like the flapping of wings.

If the bird has suddenly swelled to a huge creature,
turn to page 70.
If it has become something else, turn to page 89.

32

You wonder about the tunnel as you cautiously go forward. Did soldiers use it during the War Between the States? Or did Indians follow it when they were fighting the early settlers? You don't know—you can only guess.

You move along the soft earth fifty or sixty feet, then you realize there is water. You tread through it as carefully as you can, hoping it will not get deeper.

You step into water ankle-deep and stop abruptly. If you go any farther—

Then you look ahead and think you see a glimmer of daylight. The water can't be deep! And as you adjust your eyes to the vague light, you realize that you're right.

Fifteen more steps, and you're once more on damp earth, ground firm enough so that your shoes do not sink down. There's a used path here and you move more rapidly.

Within minutes, you break free. Into daylight!

If you think you're completely out of the Craven place, turn to page 53.
If you suspect more problems, turn to page 77.

You cannot be certain, but you guess that she is seven or eight years old. Slowly she turns her head and looks up at you. The green eyes almost hypnotize you. When she smiles, you see the tiny dimples in her cheeks. "You want to get out."

33

It is not a question. It is a simple statement. But the low, haunting voice makes you wonder whether you've been wrong about her age. "But how?" you ask.

Without taking her eyes off you, she gradually raises her right arm and points toward a dark brown square in an otherwise gray wall. "There."

You hesitate for just a moment, still wondering about the voice, then you take three quick steps toward the square. Squinting your eyes, you can tell that it has a very narrow frame about it. You put one hand on it, gently push, and it flies open. You spy a narrow tunnel that leads to a wide stoop.

With a quick sigh of relief, you glance back at the little girl—except she is no longer there.

Turn to page 34.

34

You don't care. Without waiting another second, you scurry through the opening, step onto the stoop and stand up. You discover you're back on the porch—it extends all the way around the house.

You trot around it, scamper down the steps, and retrieve your bicycle. Never mind the storm. All you want is to get out of the Craven House. Even if you get soaking wet pushing the bike home, that beats staying in a house with strange candles, a talking bird, and a little girl who disappears.

THE END

You begin to run as fast as you can, but suddenly you come to an abrupt stop. You see the reflection of the huge bird in a mirror. It lights on your back and its claws are clinging to your T-shirt. "Flee! Be free!"

You reach back and slap at it. The bird springs up, flaps its powerful wings, and begins to fly away. You chase after it. The mirrored hallway extends another twenty feet, and then suddenly you are in total darkness. Before you can adjust your vision, you hear metal clanging against metal. You look back. A barred door has dropped behind you, and you know you're in some kind of cage.

35

Is it an animal cage? Turn to page 109.
Is it some sort of prison? Turn to page 97.

36

For a full minute it stares at you, beady little eyes hardly moving, hardly blinking. Then suddenly it raises its head, opens its beak and calls out, "Stranger, stranger!"

You swallow hard. The voice is as real as that of a person, and you wonder what kind of creature this is.

"Run!" it squawks. "Run or die!"

Turn to page 7.

Perhaps you've gotten yourself turned around, perhaps not. But you are pretty certain the right-hand door leads toward the front of the house, and that's where you want to go.

Without taking time to look ahead, you turn right and step over a low but very wide sill. You push aside the heavy drapelike curtain—and suddenly find you are not alone.

Standing beside a low desk cluttered with small boxes and rows of little lights is a huge beast of a man. His gray hair is thin and stringy, with wild

Turn to page 39.

strands falling across his face. His forehead is high, his cheeks wide, his mouth little more than a thin pink line above his chin—and his nose is just a low ridgelike mound. His eyes, however, are large—the largest you have ever seen. But they have no color, no visible pupils. They are like small, shiny mirrors.

Turn to page 8.

40

You take a deep breath and turn to the other wall. There, along two similar shelves, you see doll-like figures—two children, a man in trucker's garb, two boys in jeans with backpacks slung over their shoulders, two teenage girls in swimsuits, an old woman carrying a grocery bag.

Vaguely, you think you recognize the old woman—

You shake your head. Can't be, can't be.

The man reaches behind him and lifts an object. As he easily swings it over his head and places it on the bench to his left, you spot your bicycle.

Is the man going to repair it for you? Turn to page 11.
If you think he has other ideas, turn to page 64.

Unable to open the door without a tool, you hesitate a moment, then cross the room to the wide hearth. Kneeling there, you run your hand over the stones, hoping you'll discover a nail in a cement joint. No nail. And the huge poker is too thick to work between door and frame.

41

You reach up and run your hand over the wide mantel. At first you find only dust. Then your thumb bumps a piece of straight metal, about the length of an average nail. You attempt to pick it up but it does not move.

You stand on tiptoe but you cannot quite see it. You work your fingernail beneath it but it still won't budge. Blindly, you shove it hard to the right and it suddenly breaks loose and pivots.

You hear creaking sounds coming from the opposite end of the fireplace and before you can do anything but stare, a shallow bookcase slides away. You quickly step around the hearth to see what has been revealed.

If you believe it's some kind of treasure hideaway, turn to page 104.
If you expect to find a hidden passage, turn to page 92.

42

Poised to run if the bird spreads its wings, you stare hard at the creature. But it does not move from the perch. Only its head shifts as it extends its neck to stare at you better.

Suddenly, it opens its long beak. "Intruder! Intruder!"

You don't believe what you're hearing. Parrots can talk; you've heard them. And in one of your classes a teacher told you about a man who lived in the woods and had taught a crow to say a few words. Nobody really believed that. But this bird—

"Flee for your life! Flee for your life!"

You suddenly shake all over. Never mind what you believed before—this bird can say more than simple words!

When it doesn't leave the perch, however, you ease from the chair. Maybe it will just stay where it is long enough for you to make it to the front door. If you can just get back on the wide porch you'll be happy to wait out the storm there.

Continue.

You stand slowly, eyeing the bird all the while, and gradually take a small step. The bird does not move. You take another step, and another. And while it still remains on its perch, you reach the door. Without looking, you feel for the handle.

No handle.

Frightened, you glance at the door panel. There really is no handle. The wood is smooth and blank. You're trapped.

43

If you hear the bird again, turn to page 9.
If you look for another avenue of escape, turn to page 60.

44

You see the other hand moving to catch you about the waist, but you wriggle to the side, forcing him to bend over. As he does, you jab one finger into his left eye.

What you feel is not soft but rock hard, as if the eye is a smooth piece of glass. The whole thing collapses with your punch and the man screams in agony.

He grabs his face with both hands and you are freed for the moment. Without waiting for him to reach for you again, you spin to the left and dart toward a ray of light that appears to be leaking through a crack on the other side of the room. You bang into the small wall. It gives, and you find a very narrow passageway.

Three rapid steps and you see a steep staircase. You don't know where it leads but as long as it's away from the evil man you don't care.

You're halfway up the stairs when you hear the sudden whisper-swish of something brushing against your cheek. The noise passes you, turns, and comes toward you from the back. Before you can make another move, you feel sharp toe-like claws resting on your scalp.

Turn to page 29.

Suddenly the girl screams. You can't tell whether it's a frightened call or an angry scream at you, but you give her a long look. She gradually turns back into a young child, with smooth face and beautiful hair. Her mouth is open but you see no fangs. And the snake has curled itself about her neck.

Frightened as you are, you frantically grab a pair of cooking tongs from the counter. With a lunge, you grab the snake's head and mash it. The creature swiftly unwinds itself and the girl darts away. "Help me escape!" she begs.

You drop the snake into a large bucket, tongs and all, and grab her hand. "Which way?"

She spins you about and points toward a narrow door. "There—I think."

45

Is she leading you to safety? If you think so, turn to page 50. If you suspect a trap, turn to page 57.

46

You can't be certain how many floors you've passed, but you are out of breath when you finally reach the top. You stop and lean against the wall, gasping for air. Certain that the old man will follow you, however, you stumble forward on the bare floor, feeling thick cobwebs wrapping themselves about your face and shoulders. The bird hops once, caws, "Flee for your life! You'll die!" and flies off.

Dropping to your knees, you crawl across a musty, dust-covered floor to the first wall you can touch and lean heavily against it.

But before you can relax, you feel the wall move. You tense up, lean away, and gingerly put your hand to the dirty surface. You push gently, then harder.

The wall moves an inch, then another. And as you continue to push, the board creaks and gives way entirely. There before you is a room hardly larger than a closet, with one cracked windowpane. Water has seeped through and is dripping on the floor. You stare hard—

Continue.

And you think your stomach is going to leap through your throat. Before you, hunched against the tight little corner, is the skeleton of a man still clothed in a soldier's uniform.

Frightened but desperately curious, you extend one finger and touch the nearest sleeve.

A low moan comes from somewhere.

Do you stay in the room? Turn to page 72.
Do you flee at once? Turn to page 65.

48

Since you know it's discourteous to enter someone else's house without their knowledge, you decide to seek the source of the noise. The owner is probably running an appliance of some sort.

You cross the large room and enter a wide, unlighted hall. You turn at the end and go toward the right, which is where the noise seems to come from. At the end of another short hall, you turn left, push open a swinging door, and find yourself in a room filled with all sorts of electrical devices—TV monitor screens, weird radios, electronic control boxes, a huge panel that appears to have a hundred knobs and switches. Standing beside the panel is a grotesque robot, not solid but made of wires and steel tubes.

The head, if you could call it that, turns at your entrance. One eyelike light shines in your face, so intense that you feel it burning. You take a step toward the big robot and it emits an eerie shriek. Its arms flail the air, then both reach for the control panel. Wires where a man's fingers would be flick switches, turn dials, and press three buttons.

Continue.

The first button turns on a sun-shaped lamp in the ceiling, and the second sets the lamp in motion, swinging it around until it focuses on you.

The third button creates some kind of sizzling electrical whir. At once you feel it boring into your forehead. You grab at the spot. The beam shifts, the whir gets louder, and the focus is now on your chest.

Suddenly you cannot breathe. You feel your heart beating faster and faster. Until the beats run together. And you fall. . . .

THE END

50

She grabs your hand and together you dart through the small opening—to find yourselves in a very narrow, darkened hallway. At first it seems quite long, but you and she have taken only ten or eleven steps when she suddenly moves ahead and disappears.

Two more steps and you crash into a padded wall that you had not expected. For a moment you are stunned, but while you are standing there you see two small doorways, one to the right and the other to the left. You don't have any idea where the child has gone, but you are more concerned at the moment with your own safety.

If you think the door to the left will lead you out, turn to page 19.
If you believe the right-hand door is better, turn to page 37.

Stunned by what you see him doing, you can barely breathe.

And all at once you understand. The vehicles were once as large and real as your bike. And the people—

You spin about in time to see the man take the very small bike from the machine and deftly place it on the toy shelf. Then he turns slowly, and you know you're to be the next victim of those long arms, the huge switch, and the sparks.

"No!"

You take a quick step to the right, whirl, and head toward the ray of light coming through a crack in the wall between the rows of shelves.

But you're not quite quick enough.

The man's bony fingers lock themselves on your shoulder.

Does he lift you? Turn to page 68.
Do you struggle and escape? Turn to page 44.

52

The statue room would be better than this beetle trap!

You fumble around and get halfway turned, then realize that you're cornered. They are no longer moving hither and thither. They're forming lines, like columns of marchers. They have spotted you and are moving straight at you.

You back away as far as you can—right into a locked door. You cannot escape!

You reach out, intent on smashing the first creature that draws near—but as your hand stretches forth the leader grabs your thumb. Another catches your little finger in vicious pincers.

You scream at the pain and try to roll away. But before you can do more than turn on your side they are all over you—glowing green beetles with razor-sharp pincers cutting through your clothes, impatiently looking for skin. . . .

THE END

For a moment you are relieved and start to yell with excitement. Then suddenly you catch yourself. Clear weather? Cloudy—but no rain? No lightning or wind or thunder?

And the browning grass all about—you don't recognize any of it. This close to home you should see some rolling ground, lots of trees.

Then you hear it—the low *thump-thump-thump* of strange drums. You look toward the sound. And a tightness draws up in your throat. You see a clearing, a large bonfire, huge forked stakes at either end, a long pole suspended between them, and a huge bubbling caldron suspended over the blaze. Thick blue-gray steam is curling from it.

And around the fire are strange little men. You fix your gaze on them. Pygmies!

Turn to page 55.

In America? In South Carolina? Just outside North Charleston? Can't be. But there they are, clad in loincloths and nothing else, with frightening painted stripes on their faces and bodies.

While you stare at them you suddenly feel two sharp pricks at your back. You look right and left. Two of their numbers have slipped up behind you and are now gouging you with the points of their sharp spears.

Turn to page 81.

56

Scrambling to your feet, you wheel about. The figure with the ax is no longer smiling, no longer laughing. But it has stepped around the altar and is moving toward you, ax held high. You remain motionless until it is within half a yard of you, then you suddenly roll backward, at the same time kicking as hard and as high as you can.

You can't be sure where you hit the creature, but you hear the ax clatter on the stone floor. You regain your balance, once more drop to crouching position, and look about.

You don't believe it—

But the tiny room has vanished. You're on damp, smooth dirt—like that under any house built on low pillars. You hastily look about and see that you're underneath the Craven House. Breathing a sigh of relief, you crawl out and wait just beneath the corner of the porch floor for the storm to end.

THE END

She takes your hand and together you push the door open, squeezing through the tight space that's barely wide enough for one person. On the other side, you find yourself in the corner of a large, barely lighted room with rows of shelves and one wall filled with the mounted heads of vicious animals.

Together you ease into the room and start across the floor toward the only opening you can see—an archway. You've taken only a few steps, though, when a brilliant light flashes. You catch your breath and whirl around.

Sitting at a long desk almost hidden in the shadows is the owner of Craven House—his long stringy hair hanging loose, his huge eyes fixed on both of you. You want to run, alone if necessary. But you are concerned for the girl.

If you decide to take care of yourself only, turn to page 96.
If you think the girl must accompany you, turn to page 73.
If you face the man, turn to page 69.

58

The swelling continues for several seconds, and just when you know your skin is about to split, the fluid flowing into your body stops. You try to lick your lips, but your tongue is so large you cannot get it through your teeth. You attempt to look at the creature, but your eyes are swollen shut. You want to take a deep breath, but your nose is so large that air can't get in.

The extension arm easily lifts you off the floor and holds you above its head. The arm draws back, now holding you as if you were a huge ball. With an effort you raise your eyelids and look up—

Into open sky!

The creature squats, appears to take aim, and tosses you straight up and through the passageway. You drift up and up and up—and you suddenly realize you're able to float.

You roll slowly in the wind and when you are face down, you realize you're about half a mile above the earth. You open your mouth to scream—

And the gas forced into you spews from your lips as from a violent jet. Your feet lower, your arms spread, and you come screaming down.

Continue.

And when you're no more than fifty feet up, you realize that you're headed for a big splash in the shark-infested Atlantic Ocean. You stare at the whitecaps, the rolling waves—

And at the four horrible shark fins cutting like huge black teeth through the dark water.

Turn to page 94.

60

Shaking all over now, you spin about and scamper across the room toward an archway leading to what you think is the dining room. You find a long table covered with a white sheet. Against the wall you see a row of chairs—maybe as many as twelve. At the opposite side of the room is a tall, glass-fronted cabinet. You stare hard at it, disbelieving what you see.

The shelves are filled with small glass boxes, each containing a bleached skeleton. Four of the skeletons appear to be those of rodents. One looks like that of a squirrel and another appears to be a bird's. Along the lowest shelf, all the boxes contain skulls of snakes, jaws wide and fangs exposed.

You remember all the stories you've heard about this house and you're sorry now you ever dared come onto the porch. You stare at the display for only a second before darting past it toward a long, darkened hallway. Then suddenly you stop.

Continue.

Sitting there in a very low chair is the prettiest little girl you have ever seen. Even in the shadows, you can see her face and hair clearly. Her hair is golden, with soft curls that fall about her shoulders. Her face is smooth and round, and her small mouth is perfectly shaped. Her eyes, though, are like magnets, drawing your attention.

They are a bright, bright green.

Turn to page 82.

62

The egg cracks a fourth time, and now you see what's within. And you scream. Its head is huge—like a pelican's, only much longer, and its beak is not fat and pouchlike. Its neck stretches up like a turkey's, except that, like the beak, it is lots longer. The body is all black. The creature begins to spread its wings. You think of the prehistoric-monster pictures you've seen and wonder how the old man created—

It spies you, bobs its head, and slowly begins to move toward you. It has cracked from the egg full-grown—and hungry. You press hard against the bars. You turn sideways, hoping to squeeze through.

The creature caws, and the sound is like a rattling roar. You struggle but you cannot slip through the space. Frantically you look about for a stick or a rock—anything to use as a defense. But you spot nothing.

The creature stops in front of you, flaps its mighty wings, stretches that ropelike neck, the huge head rising as it does so. The beak opens, the eyes glow red, and while you stand there terrified, the beak clamps onto your stomach. You had not seen them, but you can tell by the awful stabs that it has fangs. And you will be its first meal. . . .

THE END

Frantically, you drop to your knees and feel about the floor. There has to be something you can use to protect yourself. Your fingers touch something; you think it's an old fireplace poker. You grab it, spin about, and face the lion. It stops, seems to hesitate, then crouches—and you know it is about to spring at you. You stand stock-still, watching its forepaws. And just as it moves, you drop to the floor and roll hard to the right.

The lion-like thing crashes into a huge wooden beam that was directly behind you. It explodes, and the sound is deafening. The crash blasts a gaping hole in the roof. Splintered chunks of wood fall all about you. And the huge beam comes to rest with one end on the floor, the other protruding through the hole in the roof.

You let out a triumphant yell, grab the beam, and shinny up it as if it were a tree in your yard. Once on the roof, you slide along it until you find a rusty downspout. With one backward glance to make sure none of the headless creatures is following, you grab the downspout and slide down.

And you're outside—away from Craven House— free! You run through the yard, grab your wrecked bike, and drag it toward the road.

After that experience, who cares about a storm?

THE END

64

As he sets it upright you realize that it is as good as new and you wonder how it got fixed. Your gaze shifts once more to the row of doll creatures. They're too real, too lifelike. The old woman's dress is wrinkled and limp as though from a walk on a hot day. The trucker's shirt, halfway unbuttoned, is stained with perspiration, and the stubble of beard is quite real. It is the backpackers' hair, though, that really catches your attention—how could an artist make that so real?

You hear a low buzz from the workbench. The man has hooked a long metal arm to the bicycle's rear wheel, another to the handlebars. He adjusts two knobs on the metal arms, grunts, and flicks a large switch.

Sparks at once shower around the bicycle and you step away, wondering if you're going to be burned by them. But they do not come near you.

Within moments the bicycle is no larger than the toylike items on the shelf.

Turn to page 51.

The sound makes you tremble all over. You can't tell where it came from but you don't want to stay here. You whip about and grab the tiny door and scurry through it. Whatever's downstairs, it can't be any worse than a moaning ghost-soldier.

You start tiptoeing down the stairs and are halfway to the bottom when once more the black bird swoops just over your head. It caws once, circles, and glides to a perch on your shoulder. Its long beak nips at your ear. "Follow me! I'll set you free!"

You know it's silly but you talk back to it. "Show me! Just show me how to get out of Craven House!"

The bird flies down to the bottom of the staircase, suddenly swerves back, and perches on the handrail five steps from the landing. With its right wing it brushes against the wall. "Follow me—free!"

Hopefully you run your hand over the seemingly blank wall. You touch a knothole and jam your finger into it.

There's a button of some sort hidden inside! You push hard.

A section of the wall opens and you find a wide, candle-lighted hall. With the bird on your shoulder again, you hastily step through the opening and onto the carpeted floor. At once the wall slams shut.

If you follow the bird, turn to page 31.
If you try to turn back, turn to page 75.
If you proceed on your own, turn to page 85.

66

You are sure that whoever is coming will reach the room before you can find a hiding place, so you quickly decide to slip into the closet. Perhaps there is more room than you can see; maybe you can press against the back of the bookcase.

Still holding the little candle, you slip through the narrow opening.

But the moment you do, the bookcase slowly closes. And you are within the closet.

The candlelight flickers and sputters. But your attention is drawn to the knife display, for as the bookcase slides into place, you hear a sharp click. Every knife flicks to an upright position—triggered, you realize, by the sliding case.

You are terrified. You realize those knives are mounted on a board that is beginning to move toward you—and within moments they will be sticking in you—

You scream! But there is no sound; your throat is paralyzed.

Continue.

As you stare at the knife points, you begin to hear a buzzing noise. The blades are beginning to work up and down, like many saws. Not only will they stick you—they'll saw away at your body!

You make one quick move, turning sideways and pressing your back against the rear of the bookcase. And you're just clear of the closet blades! One of them slashes your shirtfront.

You take a deep breath and hug the wall. The knife board continues moving.

Turn to page 76.

68

For a second your whole body goes tense and you try to twist yourself free. But you suddenly feel one of the man's fingers extend beyond your shoulder to a spot at the center of your neck. He presses hard.

You feel intense pain. Then nothing.

You are awake, you know he is lifting you off the floor, you know he is placing you over his worktable, and you dimly see the long metal arms he used on the bicycle. Almost hypnotized, you watch as he attaches one of them to your ankles, the other to your hands. He turns a crank you cannot see clearly, and you find yourself being stretched and stretched.

You are extended straight out and he pivots the machine to place you directly over the table, suspended.

You feel the first shock as the electricity enters your body. Sparks fly. And as you drift to sleep you feel yourself shrinking. . . .

THE END

Although you are very frightened, you turn and face the old man. "Let me leave. Let us both leave."

He throws back his wrinkled head and cackles a laugh. "I love wee ones!" The voice is shrill and cutting. "I keep wee ones!"

69

"Not me!" you yell at him. "Not us!"

The girl shakes all over and her knees begin to buckle. You cling to her hand, holding her up. Still keeping your gaze fixed on the old man's face, you begin easing toward the narrow door, dragging the girl. Just as you near it, however, and are reaching for a tiny latch, the floor beneath you suddenly gives way.

Turn to page 87.

70

What you hear are sounds like chains rattling together, and there are clacking sounds, also, as though metal were striking the ground.

The noise comes nearer, and the reflected light from the huge eyes illuminates the walls. In the blinding light you see a monstrous apelike man with gigantic arms and legs. On its huge hands are metal gloves and its feet are covered with boot-shaped metal plates.

You wonder, is this the insane genius who owns Craven House?

Or is this something the madman has created?

The creature moves with mechanical steps. Suddenly he stops. One hand raises and the index finger points at you. From the tip of the finger a thin metal rod with a star-shaped tip begins to extend.

Seconds later, the star has become a five-pointed extension of crooked fingers. They suddenly spring forward and lock themselves about your head. As their tips dig into your skin you feel liquid begin to flow through you. Your face starts to swell, then your neck, then your stomach.

Turn to page 99.

72

You turn quickly and look toward the window. Nothing there.

Again you glance at the skeleton. Timidly you extend one hand to touch the dry skull. A spark flies and you jerk back. Then very slowly, right there before your eyes, a form begins to take shape. It is as transparent as molded glass. The uniform begins to swell. One shoe scrapes across the bare floor and one arm falls limply to the side.

The head and body grow to normal proportions. But the face is featureless—no nose, no mouth, no eyes. Only low bumps where the brows and nose should be.

The figure moves ever so slightly. The moan comes once more.

You don't care how hard it's raining. With two quick, hard kicks you knock the cracked windowpane from its frame, duck low, and scamper through it to the steep roof. You don't care about the wind and lightning. You don't care about anything but getting out. You'll stay there and yell and yell and yell. *But you won't go back inside* . . . .

THE END

73

You're not sure what the girl is doing in the house, but you feel her fingers trembling and decide she is as frightened as you are. You hesitate only a moment before turning toward the little door through which you entered the room.

"Renette!"

The sound echoes through the room as the old man yells. The child shakes all over—you can feel her arm almost vibrate. She screams: "No! No, no!"

Renette? Not "Peggy"? But no matter. You move to put yourself between her and the desk and as you do so, you brush a book stand. Lying on it is a stack of loose papers and a rocklike paperweight. Without hesitating, you grab the heavy object and hold it high.

The old man laughs. The sound is weird, reminding you of an owl's cry on a dark night. You hurl the missile at the man's head. He ducks and totters out of the chair. He groans once and sprawls on the floor.

You think you hit him but you aren't taking any chances. Still clutching the girl's hand, you scamper through the archway.

Turn to page 103.

74

Suddenly you notice the back of the small closet has opened and there before you is another hallway. This one is plain and uncluttered, longer than you might have expected.

You hurry down it, hoping the footsteps don't follow you. At the far end you find a door and push through it. And you're in the largest kitchen you believe you've ever seen. It has a huge counter that is three times as long as the one at your house, a giant wood-burning stove, a refrigerator that is as large as your home bathroom, and all kinds of electrical gadgets along the wall. A man-sized robot is standing before the stove, cooking thick, steaming stew.

The robot ignores you and you slip around it. You mean to look for a rear door. But just as you pass the refrigerator you hear a soft sound.

Does it come from the refrigerator? Turn to page 12.
From somewhere else? Turn to page 107.

The bird caws once more. "Flee! Be free!" It swoops low over your head, flies in a tight circle, and glides rapidly along the hallway.

And it disappears.

The moment it gets out of sight you feel a violent gust of wind blowing at you. It howls and swirls about you, raising the carpet and flinging it about like a flimsy sheet on a clothesline. And all the candles go out at once. You are in total darkness.

For a moment you stand still, trying to see ahead. As you peer, straining to catch a glimpse of the floor, the carpet wraps itself about you. The howling changes to voices that rise and fall on the wind: "Down, down you go. Down to the burning place!"

You are very frightened. The bird is leading you into some kind of trap.

Without waiting for any other sound, you whirl about and feel for the opening. Your fingers slide nervously along the surface of the boards, seeking the passageway. Nothing.

The carpet continues to swirl, knotting itself and flapping at your back. You grab for a corner of it— and discover it is slippery. Your fingers cannot hold it.

Turn to page 83.

76

It reaches the opposite wall and begins cutting away. You cannot believe what you're seeing—but the knives are literally sawing through the wall!

Within seconds you see daylight!

Daylight! And you don't care whether it's raining or storming or thundering—all you can think about is daylight!

As the huge board of knife-saws bashes and cuts through the wall and begins to chew into the porch, you swing wildly to the right. The nearest knife cuts your sleeve.

But you jerk free just in time—

And you're on the porch and you scamper to your bicycle and grab the handlebars. Never mind the bent wheel—you're free!

You're out of the Craven House—but nobody will believe how you escaped!

THE END

Daylight?

Not really. It may seem that way because everything is so bright, but the minute you look around, you realize you're back inside the Craven House. The brilliance is from more shining bulbs than you have ever seen in one place before. You think of operating rooms in hospitals—

You choke back a quick cry.

This *is* an operating room. You see the table, you see silvery instruments arranged on a gleaming tray, you see oxygen tanks and tubes, you see a machine that looks like an X-ray device, you see a large box of bandaging material—

And you see the tall figure of a man dressed in white, his face covered by a mask, his head almost entirely wrapped in cloth, rubber gloves on his hands.

Turn to page 78.

78

Before you can move, four long mechanical arms reach down from the ceiling and lift you. They turn you about and place you on the table. While two of the arms hold you in position, the other two bring up wide beltlike bands and strap you down. One of the arms brings a cuplike device over your face and clamps it so that both your mouth and nose are encased.

The man—his eyes are more frightening than any you've ever seen—reaches to the left and picks up one of the sharp silvery instruments. "First," he says in a shrill voice, "we must remove the vital part—the brain. . . ."

THE END

Frightened curiosity leads you to take a closer look. You take slow steps across the floor, your footsteps echoing as you move. You stop beside the bed and stare down. Although the body does not move, the eyes are wide open. You stare at them—and look through the clear pupils into a void that you do not understand.

You decide to run, but you cannot. You feel paralyzed. You can only stare, dumbfounded.

And while you stare, a rasping whisper comes from the form. "Come be with me."

Turn to page 80.

80

Urgently you will yourself to run. But it's no use; you seem to be frozen in your tracks.

When you see the small motion you want to spin away. But you do not.

A long, flabby-fleshed arm comes out from beneath the sheet. A gnarled hand stretches for you. Black fingernails dig into your wrist. "Come with me."

You try to back away. You cannot.

"Come sleep. As I must sleep. *For-ev-er.*"

THE END

They force you to walk toward the fire and the caldron. And when you're within ten feet of them, one of their numbers breaks from the shelter of a clump of tall brush. He is larger than the others, about as tall as you. His chest, arms, and legs have the white pattern of a skeleton painted over them. A string of beads—teeth?—dangles from his neck. His headpiece is that of a crocodile, and he does an ominous little dance as he moves toward you.

Their chief? Or medicine man?

He approaches until the outer lips of the headpiece are only inches from your face. He makes a low guttural sound. The mouth opens wide, and a roar comes from it.

And before you can move, four of the pygmies rush you. Although you struggle and flail your arms, they quickly lift you. They stretch you out, bind you to a long pole, and carry you toward the fire.

There they pause long enough to set you upright. Then, while all the others intone an eerie chant, they lift you and stand you up in the caldron's boiling oil.

THE END

82

As you stare at her, you think you recognize the face. Three weeks ago a little girl disappeared from Monk's Corner. You didn't know her but her picture was in the paper and on TV. You're not sure, but you think her name was Peggy—Peggy something.

But what is she doing here? Did she run away and come to this house to hide from her parents? Or did she just come inside the Craven House—as you did—to get out of a storm? And if so, is she a captive? Has somebody turned her into—into what? A little witch?

Or is she just as afraid as you are—but they've hypnotized her?

If the girl jumps up and runs from you, turn to page 27.
If she smiles at you, turn to page 33.

As the carpet gathers about you, you draw your knees up till they touch your chin. You are curled in a ball, and the carpet suddenly begins to swing back and forth, as if held by a rope you cannot see.

You know if you don't do something soon, the thing will bang you against a wall if it keeps swinging.

The carpet, though, is old—probably rotten. It will tear—you know it'll tear.

You hold your breath. And just as the carpet swings you hard to where you remember the wall was, you kick with all your might.

Great! The old carpet rips and you fall forward— right through the wall—which is nothing more than cardboard!

But you keep falling!

Turn to page 108.

84

Maybe you can—

Before you have time to think about it, the creature is within a foot of where you are huddled. Its tongue extends all the way, and comes within an inch of your knee.

You hesitate only a moment before leaping as hard as you can to the right.

The creature is slower, although it follows you with its frightening gaze. You move to the side, stare hard, and kick its underside as hard as you can.

A shrill cry breaks from the creature's small mouth. It trembles all over.

You kick again, this time even harder.

It screams once more, it shakes even harder. And its powerful tail wraps around a bar of the cage. As the creature sways with pain, the bars begin to spread, creating a wide space.

Before you is a straight, wide tunnel. At the far end you see light. Without waiting, you squeeze through the bars, and run as hard as you can toward the stormy weather outside this crazy house. . . .

THE END

But you are no sooner within the passageway than the bird speeds up and disappears. And you're on your own.

You walk fifty, maybe sixty feet before you reach a huge black door with a brass latch. You touch it—

And an alarm rings!

The old man who lives in this place must be an electronic engineer—maybe a genius. But whatever he is, you don't wait to see what the alarm causes.

Once more you push the latch. It lifts, then slides back and the door swings open. You quickly step through and onto soft earth. Just as you thought—a tunnel. You release the door and it slowly closes. Once it's shut, you are in total darkness.

You walk slowly, feeling your way with your feet, but as you move, you realize the ground is getting softer and softer. You think about underground rivers, about quicksand and dismal swamps.

What is this? Turn to page 32.

86

You jerk back your fingers, trembling all over. Real people! Real people encased in modeling clay!

You realize that staying here is unsafe. So, shaking all over, you move from the statue and look about the room. All you see, other than the entry, is a small door on the far side of the wall. You can't tell where it leads, but if it will get you out of here, that's fine.

You rush toward it and have to bend over to get through. You bump your head but keep going. On the other side of the little door you find only a crawl space, so you drop to your knees. You wonder about such a narrow opening, but it's so dark you have no way of knowing where it will lead.

You crawl about fifteen feet, then abruptly you stop. You spot small blobs of glowing green light—and you stop breathing when you realize they're coming from crawling creatures. You stare hard, adjusting your vision to the dimness. Only then do you realize what the creatures are—beetles, huge, vicious beetles as big as rats, with long, wicked-looking pincers.

Turn to page 52.

Together you drop onto a curving sliding board that speeds you rapidly through a pitch-black tunnel. You swing right and left and right again before both of you tumble onto a flat, soft landing. You spring to your feet, dragging the little girl with you. "We'd better run," you tell her.

"I can't see!"

You can't see, either. But you begin to run straight ahead, hoping there's nothing in the way. You don't, however, get very far, as moments later you bump into something low and both of you trip over it. As you scramble to your feet, a double row of flickering lights comes on. They sparkle red and blue, red and blue. And they cast a faint glow all around. You both stare at them and discover that they surround a carved box, long and narrow. To your horror, you realize that it's an open coffin.

Turn to page 88.

88

Before you can do anything to stop her, the child hops into the box and lies down.

And a very weird change occurs. She grows longer. Her features change. Her hair gets dark. Her dress changes to black. And even while you stare, terrified by the sight, she becomes your Aunt Marsha.

And a deep, throaty laugh echoes around you as one hand reaches out, clasps you about the neck, and drags you in beside her. . . .

THE END

The sound is that of metal and wires scraping together. You desperately want to spin about and run. But for some reason you cannot move.

The thing moves toward you and as it nears, you feel a slight tingling through your body. When it is within a foot of where you stand, it halts. The noise suddenly dies. And a strange brown glow spreads through the passage.

89

Turn to page 91.

In the ghostlike light you begin to make out the object. Strands of coiled barbed wire and pieces of pipe, lengths of narrow metal bands and round rusty disks have somehow joined to form the most frightening creature you can imagine.

The tingling gets worse and you think of electricity running through your body.

91

Turn to page 20.

92

A hidden stairway! You're not really surprised because old houses like this one often have secret halls and doors. You step quickly through the opening. As you do so, your leg brushes a long lever. At once the bookcase slides back into place. You're trapped.

Frantically you scamper up the steps. They take you into a large, empty room on the next floor—empty, except for a huge picture that takes up one entire wall. The picture is of an old battlefield late in the evening, with dead and dying soldiers lying all around. It's frightening and you don't like it.

You decide to go back down the steps, but before you can, something eerie happens. The battlefield seems to move. The soldiers on the ground become three-dimensional. The room becomes filled with the real scene. You can even smell gunsmoke and something worse that smells horrible.

You take a step back—and fall onto the form of a prone soldier. He's dead! You can't help screaming.

Continue.

And when you scream, you hear a groan. You look to the left. A badly wounded soldier staggers to his feet, yells something you do not understand, and charges toward you.

The room is too small. There's nowhere to run. Before you can whirl toward the stairway, the attacker reaches you. He pulls the trigger of his long rifle. It does not fire. He yells once more, draws back the weapon, and jabs you in the stomach with the deadly bayonet. . . .

THE END

94

Oh, no!

Frantically you grab your nose with one hand, clap the other over your mouth.

You don't splash down. By stopping the jet flow, you've made yourself into a hovering balloon.

You want to yell—but you dare not open your mouth.

You want to breathe, but you dare not move your hand from your nose.

Then suddenly a vicious wind, blowing from the ocean, throws you wildly toward the shore.

You do not move either hand until you see trees below you.

Then, when you open your mouth and free your nose to let the jet force escape, you plummet down— to crash in the top branches of a very tall tree.

And there you must wait out the storm. . . .

THE END

The cylinder comes lower and lower and you feel the sudden impact of sticky clay coming down on your head. You try to turn but you cannot. You try to scream but you cannot.

The child-witch laughs, but there is no mirth in the sound.

95

THE END

96

Right now is no time to ask questions. Besides, you're sure the man won't answer.

And the girl—what did she say her name was? She didn't, but you have the distinct feeling that they are somehow related. Maybe she's his daughter, although he seems quite old. Or maybe she is his granddaughter.

Of course, she could belong to somebody else, some other family, and be trapped here as you seem to be. She could be that girl Peggy. But whatever, you can't help her if you don't first help yourself.

You ease away from her and sidle toward the opposite wall. Without looking, you feel along it, reaching for some kind of curtain or door—anything that protects an opening. Luckily, in the center you brush against a small handle. Blindly you grab and turn it. Stepping backward, you find yourself in another long hallway—but this one is so brightly lighted that you have to blink your eyes.

You let the door slam shut and spin around. The hallway has mirrored walls, zigzagging along a path that seems to lead directly away from the room where the man is sitting at his desk.

Turn to page 35.

You cry out and grab the bars. But before you can do more than shake them, the cage begins to rise. It goes up slowly, like a freight elevator. You don't know whether it's fastened to a cable or is being pushed up by some strange device. But however it's done, the thing carries you higher and higher. You cannot believe what's happening! That old man must be crazy! He has to be!

Abruptly the movement stops. Perhaps you're going to be let out—

Then you hear them—wild dogs howling!

Turn to page 98.

98

You didn't feel any movement other than rising but you must have been carried to the back of the house. Yet it's too dark—you're still inside the building.

The howling gets louder. You squint hard, trying to see. You spot a long, sloping tunnel; the cage is at the end of it. And while you stare, the dogs appear.

Their yellow eyes glow, their long, red tongues drip saliva, and their pointed teeth are bared. They snarl, they snap at one another. And the pack moves toward you.

But the cage will protect you—

The cage will *not* protect you!

For the side nearest the tunnel opens and the largest of the dogs leaps at you. . . .

THE END

"Never enter Craven House!"

You can't tell where the voice comes from, but you say to yourself that if you can ever get out of this place, you'll never, never come to Craven House again.

For several seconds you continue to swell, and you wonder if you'll burst into a hundred fragments or if somehow the swelling will suddenly stop and you can shrink to your normal size.

If you continue to swell, turn to page 58.
If you stop swelling and begin to shrink, turn to page 106.

100

You stare up inside the cylinder and are terrified to see hundreds of small nozzlelike jets protruding from its inner wall. Instinctively, you know what it is. That thing will come down over you, smother you, and spray wet clay all over you.

It will turn you into a statue.

Slowly the cylinder lowers. You gaze from it to the child. The soft, smooth, smiling face is changing before your eyes. Wrinkles now crease the cheeks.

Turn to page 102.

102

The eyes seem to sink deeper, the hair turns to lank gray, the nose stretches and the mouth is open. Fangs touch her lower lip.

You try to pull your arm away from her but the bony, steel-like fingers dig into your flesh.

Turn to page 95.
OR
Turn to page 115.

Luckily it leads you back to the main room, and as you pass the first large chair, you feel something in the floor give slightly. You stop short, thinking it's another trap. But when the front door swings open you realize you've accidentally stepped on the secret release button.

You dart through the door. And just in time, too, for it slams shut at once.

But you don't care. You are out! And the little girl is with you. She slumps to the floor. You start to bend over, then stop, wondering if this is another frightening trick. Maybe she is really a witch, maybe it only *looks* like the porch. . . .

She peers up at you, tears streaming from her face. "I—my name's not Renette," she says between sobs. "I got lost when it stormed and went inside to hide. That—that man caught me and turned me into a—" she choked on the word.

"A witch?" you ask.

"A witch," she mutters. "Please—*please* take me to Mommy and Daddy."

You take hold of her hand once more. "I will," you say softly. "Don't cry—you don't have to cry any longer."

THE END

104

As you draw near, you discover a darkened area about the size of your mother's linen closet. But the inside is black and the soft glow from the candles does not light it well. You touch the walls and discover they are lined with very soft cloth. To hide something? Or to deaden sound?

Furtively looking about to make certain no one has entered the room, you take one of the candles and hold it within the space. You cannot believe what you see.

Rows and rows of long knives face you. All kinds—daggers, bayonets, swords, even very thin stilettos. You are so surprised and curious you reach for one without thinking.

But the moment your hand gets within the dark space, a shower of sparks explodes from the ceiling and causes the whole closet to glow. At the same time a siren goes off and the piercing sound fills the house.

You wheel about, groping for the nail-like switch to close the bookcase. You can't find it . . . and suddenly you hear heavy footsteps.

If you duck within the closet-like area, hoping not to be seen, turn to page 66.
If you choose to flee, turn to page 74.

Then very abruptly you open them again. Something has moved, something has happened to the chair.

It's sinking! Right there in the room—and it's sinking!

You try to scramble up but before you can do more than kick out one foot, you and the chair are both below floor level.

"Hey!"

But nobody responds to your cry.

The chair keeps going down and down—and in less than a minute you're in a room that looks like a very tiny church—except that on the walls are pictures of ghouls and witches and devil-shaped creatures. At the front of the room is a long, low altar.

The chair halts and from behind the altar a figure rises. It has the face of Satan but its one long horn is at the center of its forehead. In its hands is an executioner's ax. The creature laughs!

Without waiting another second, you spring from the chair, whirl around and run as hard as you can away from the altar. You bang headlong into a wall and fall back.

105

Turn to page 56.

106

Suddenly the swelling stops. At once you begin to shrink.

You return to your normal size and are beginning to breathe a sigh of relief.

But the shrinking continues.

You're as small as you were when you were eight. You're as small as you were when you were five.

But you don't want to get any smaller!

You yell and whirl about. "Stop it! Stop it!"

But you continue getting littler and littler . . . and as you're shrinking, you hear a snarl. You look toward the sound.

The most vicious-looking black cat you have ever seen is stalking you. Its eyes glow red, its whiskers are like long needles, its fur is like dreadful straw, and its sharp teeth shine!

You take one tiny step, and the cat is upon you.

THE END

107

As you glance toward the refrigerator, you hear the sound again. Footsteps—soft, childlike footsteps. A little girl comes in from a side door. She smiles when she sees you. Without a word, she takes your hand and leads you from the kitchen to the very large dining room. An old man is sitting at one end of the table and you wonder how he got there. You cannot see his eyes because he is wearing dark glasses. The girl points to a chair and tells you to be seated.

You're not hungry but you are afraid to say no. The man looks at the girl, then at you, nods his head and presses a small button beside his plate.

At once, a wide serving table rolls in from the kitchen. On it are three large bowls of stew, blue steam rising from them. The man looks at all three, then selects one for the girl, one for himself. He hesitates a moment before passing the third one to you.

Turn to page 16.

108

You can't guess how far you have fallen before you tumble into something soft and musty. You squat and roll over twice before you stop. You pause where you are, catching your breath, and quickly look around. You discover you're in a tunnel and light is seeping through.

Daylight!

You scamper along the dirt floor, keeping low, and when you reach the end, you're in the Craven House backyard!

Out and away!

THE END

109

An animal cage! It has to be some sort of animal cage. The heavy bars remind you of the enclosures for lions and tigers at the zoo you once visited.

You cringe and slowly turn around. In the far corner, surrounded by a soft orange glow, you spot an egg-shaped object—but it is the largest egg you have ever seen. You wonder if the man who owns the house has used some of his electronic wizardry to make a plain chicken egg grow to such a giant size.

The thing emits a harsh cracking noise. You stare hard, holding your breath.

It cracks again. And again.

That cannot be a chicken—not even a huge one. You think about snakes—some of them lay eggs. And spiders—maybe he has worked with spider eggs.

One end of the giant egg pops open, and you crouch, watching. All you can see is something black and leathery. And maybe a little shiny.

A snake? Turn to page 24.
Some other kind of creature? Turn to page 62.

110

You are about to reach farther up the arm, wondering if the clay will break there, also. But just as you begin to move your hand you hear a low, scraping noise.

You turn toward the center of the room and there you spot a pedestal like the ones on which the other statues are mounted, except this one is low and flat. And while you are staring at it you hear soft footsteps.

Looking to the left you see a little girl, smiling and walking toward you. How did she get in? You did not hear a door open. And who is she, anyway?

Before you have time to think about this, she comes to you and puts her hand on your wrist. As she does so, you are quite surprised to realize how long her fingers are—they reach all around your arm!

Wordlessly, she begins to lead you toward the pedestal. You think about resisting but do not. When you reach it, she motions for you to step onto it.

And the moment you do, you feel yourself going stiff all over. You can barely move your head. But a cracking noise comes from the ceiling and you look up. There, just above you, a pipelike cylinder is descending. It is large enough to cover you.

If you struggle but cannot move, turn to page 100.
If you force yourself to move, turn to page 112.

You whirl about and look at the child. The face is tearless, the eyes are shining, the cheeks are all wrinkled, and the pretty hair is gray and stringy. She laughs and you see horrid fangs.

And before you can move she slams the refrigerator door shut.

In the darkness you begin to shiver. You know you are here for good.

THE END

112

Using all the strength you have left, you make one wild, frantic lunge and jerk free of the girl's hand. She screams at you. You look at her and see her change—wrinkles crease her face, the hair turns stringy, the mouth opens to expose fangs, the arms and hands wither, the fingers grow even longer and bony.

You spin around and spot one lone window looking out onto the roof of the porch. With a little cry, you charge toward it.

But as you pass the girl, she leaps onto your back, locks her arms about your neck and digs her heels into your sides. Once more she screams.

You don't care if she does cling to your back—she's not going to stop you. Running as hard as you can, you crash headlong into the window.

It doesn't shatter.

It doesn't break at all.

But the wooden frame splinters and the whole pane falls out. You scramble through the tiny opening, with the girl still clinging to you. You slide over the rough shingles to the gutter. You grab onto it, swing out, and drop to the ground.

Continue.

The girl slides off your back and crumples to the grass. And when you look at her you see the golden hair, the pretty face. And big tears. She looks up at you, sobbing. "Thank you—oh, thank you for rescuing me. I don't like that horrid, horrid house. My name is Peggy—please take me home."

THE END

114

Once more you thank him and balance yourself on the seat. With your left foot you shove off. You've barely gotten the bicycle rolling when you hit the curtain and brush it aside—

And there before you is a huge hole in the floor. Before you can stop yourself you ride off the edge and fall and fall and fall—until you come to a sudden crashing stop.

You're in ankle-deep muddy mire with stinging, flying insects swarming all over you. Desperately, you look up. The man is above, leaning over, grinning down at you. . . .

THE END

The cylinder lowers and as you look up you feel gusts of freezing air blowing on your head. You try to scream but you cannot make a sound.

115

Then, just before the mold begins to encase you, you summon all the strength you have. You turn halfway, swing with your free arm, and lock your fingers about the child-witch's own wrist. If you are to become a statue, so is she.

She shakes all over. The expression in her eyes is one of fear. But your hand is as locked on her as hers is on you.

Just before the cylinder covers your head she screams out the most blood-chilling sound you have ever heard.

And suddenly you are alone. Outside the room. Off the pedestal. Nothing clings to your wrist. You are dazed but clearly have escaped from the descending cylinder.

You shake your head and look about. And you are more relieved than you've ever been in your life to find that you're standing on the porch of the Craven House. Outdoors, just waiting for the rain to stop so you can push your bike home . . .

THE END

116

The bird flies all around the room, going in circles that become smaller and smaller as it draws close to you. Finally, almost as if it has just spotted you, it hovers, then slowly lands on your head. Its claws dig in, burying themselves in your thick hair, the claw-tips scratching your scalp.

Clinging to you and feeling much, much bigger than you think it actually is, it commences to beat its wings once more. You cannot believe what you are feeling—but this bird is lifting you. It flies almost to the ceiling, letting you dangle limply. It turns, ducks through a doorway, and flies rapidly through several rooms to a wide staircase. Up it goes, through the second floor and on to something like a bell tower. It drops you in a huge nest—larger than your bed.

And before you can even move, it lights on your chest and drops a pellet about the size of a sunflower seed into your mouth. You don't mean to—but you swallow it.

At once you grow still. You cannot move a single muscle. All you can do is lie there and stare, frightened all over, as the black creature hops to your chin and sets itself to pecking . . .

THE END

Books in our
PLOT-YOUR-OWN HORROR STORIES™
Series!

CRAVEN HOUSE HORRORS #1
by Hilary Milton

NIGHTMARE STORE #2
by Hilary Milton